PERCY SHORT
AND
CUTHBERT
Susie Jenkin-Pearce

VIKING

In the great swamplands and grasslands of Africa live many strange and wonderful creatures, all of them different and special in their own ways.

But among these animals were two friends who hated being different. Percy Short was the TINIEST hippo you have ever seen, and his best –

and only – friend Cuthbert was an absolutely ENORMOUS pelican. They made such an odd pair that the other animals often giggled when they saw them.

One day, Cuthbert said to Percy, "I wish that there was something we could do to make us like the others."

Percy, who was very clever, and read lots of books, replied:

"There's an old tale about a plant called the Pingo-Pongo tree. It only grows on the Island on the Other Side of the World. The old tale says that whoever eats a leaf, can have one wish come true."

Cuthbert looked at Percy with shining eyes.
"We'll find it," he shouted.

So they packed Cuthbert's beak
and Percy pored over his maps and charts.
When all was ready, Percy attached his compass to Cuthbert's beak, and they set off in search of the Pingo-Pongo tree.

They had not gone far when they came to a village where all the people were weeping.

"We have a man-eating leopard prowling the jungle," said the head of the village.

"Soon it will attack us."

"Well," said Percy. "I may be small, but I am not stupid, and Cuthbert is big and very strong. I think that I may have an idea."

The two whispered together and set off back into the jungle.

A short way in, just before a small clearing,
they dug a hole.

Cuthbert hid in the undergrowth beside
the hole and only his beak
was left showing.

Percy went into the clearing and
started to dance and sing.

Soon they heard a rumbling growl.
Cuthbert opened his beak very wide and
Percy danced while the leopard padded
nearer and nearer until suddenly . . .

PLOP! He disappeared.

Cuthbert shut his bill swiftly on the leopard, and flew with him to the great river. There he opened his beak and dropped him into the deep water.

The villagers were overjoyed and begged them to stay. But Percy and Cuthbert were determined to find the Pingo-Pongo tree. They came to a desert and the sun was blisteringly hot. Percy's footsteps became slower and slower.

"I'm drying out," he gasped. "I need water."

"Don't worry," said Cuthbert. "I'll find some and bring it back in my beak." He emptied their luggage and off he flew.

Percy lay on the sand in the burning heat.
As he drifted into unconsciousness, he thought he heard a distant sound.

"Please let it be Cuthbert," he whispered.

When he awoke his skin felt cool and wet.

"Thank you, Cuth—" he began, but then gasped in horror. All that he could see were bars. He was in a cage!

"Help!" he cried. "Where am I?"

A camel train of travelling gypsies had found him in the desert and brought him to a great city.

Percy was taken to the palace. The King had never seen an animal like him before.

"Oh, Cuthbert," cried Percy. "Where are you?"

With his bill full of water, Cuthbert returned to the desert where he had left Percy. But Percy was nowhere to be seen. Flying as fast as he could, he followed the tracks left by the camel train. As he flew over the great city, he heard Percy's pitiful cry. Cuthbert swooped and scooped Percy into his bill.

He soared high into the sky, as the roars of excitement from the crowd turned into roars of rage.

On and on they flew until they had left the vast desert far behind them. Cuthbert dropped exhausted beside the ocean.

"The sea at last," he gasped.

Soon the two friends were bobbing away from the land on the endless blue waters and playing games with passing whales and dolphins.

Then they came to an island that was like nothing they had ever seen before.

A large flower leaned forward and softly said:
"Welcome to the Island on the Other Side of the World."
"We're here," shouted Cuthbert with delight, "but where is the Pingo-Pongo tree?"

The flower pointed upwards to the tip of the very highest rock.

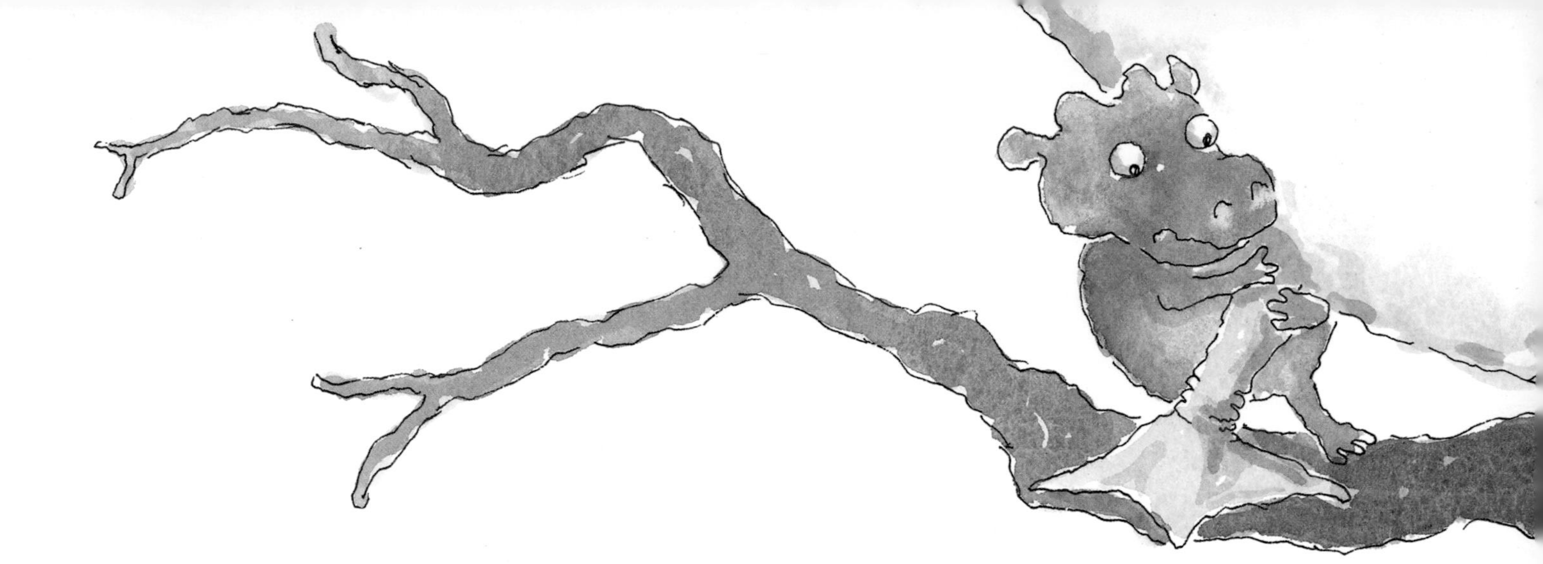

Cuthbert scooped Percy up into his bill and flew on to one of the tree's branches. Only one leaf was still hanging there! They looked at each other with dismay – only ONE WISH!

"You have it, Percy," said Cuthbert. "I know how much you long to be bigger."

"NO, you have it," replied Percy. "With a friend like you it really doesn't bother me any more. With all the adventures that we've had, I haven't thought about my size for ages. In fact, what I wish for more than anything is to be home again."

"That's exactly what I wish for, too," said Cuthbert, and they went back to the shore of the wonderful Island and found one of the friendly whales waiting to take them on board.

The whale swam at full speed back to the tropical waters near their home. As they walked through the jungle, creatures kept popping out to greet them. Word of their return soon spread and as they approached the swamps, they saw a huge banner.

OME HOME PERCY AND CUTHBERT
TRICKERS AND INTREPID EXPLORERS

Their families and friends ran out to meet them and stopped and stared in amazement.

"My goodness," they gasped. "WHAT a difference finding that Pingo-Pongo tree has made to you!"

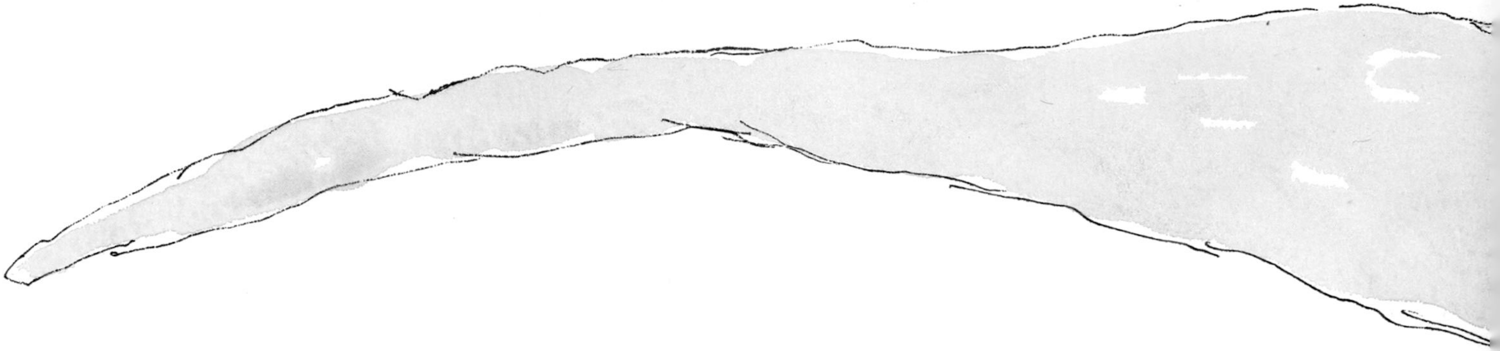

Percy and Cuthbert looked at each other knowingly.

"Yes," they said. "We think so too, and now we're back, we'll use our experiences to help anyone who comes to us with a problem – no matter how big or small."

And they did, but that's another story.

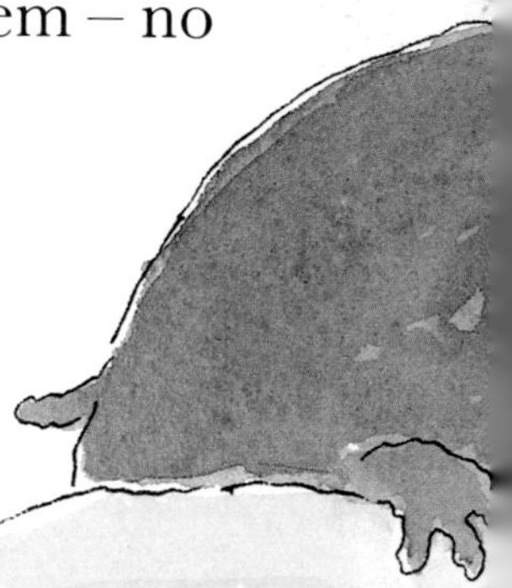

This book is specially
for Clunes, with love.

**VIKING**
Published by the Penguin Group
27 Wrights Lane, London W8 5TZ, England
Viking Penguin, a division of Penguin Books USA Inc.,
375 Hudson Street, New York, New York 10014, USA
Penguin Books Australia Ltd, Ringwood, Victoria, Australia
Penguin Books Canada Ltd, 2801 John Street, Markham, Ontario, Canada L3R 1B4
Penguin Books (NZ) Ltd, 182–190 Wairau Road, Auckland 10, New Zealand

Penguin Books Ltd, Registered Offices: Harmondsworth, Middlesex, England

First published 1990
1 3 5 7 9 10 8 6 4 2



Filmset in Baskerville by Chambers Wallace, London

Printed in Hong Kong by Imago

A CIP catalogue recorded for this book is available from the British Library
ISBN 0-670-82803-3